The
INVITATION
～ Nicola Smee ～

Little, Brown and Company
Boston Toronto London

For
Richard and Fara
Maddy Farrell
Michael
Olly, Milo
and Leo . . .
with love

First U.S. edition

Library of Congress Catalog Card Number 89-83671

ISBN: 0-316-79894-0

10 9 8 7 6 5 4 3 2 1

First published in Great Britain in 1989 by William Collins
Sons & Co. Ltd.

Printed in Belgium by
Proost International Book Production

Next morning...